Can't Get Me!

Written By
Lisa Lynn MacDonald

Illustrated By
Madison Mastrangelo

S0-AXJ-671

AuthorHouse™
1663 Liberty Drive
Bloomington, IN 47403
www.authorhouse.com
Phone: 1-800-839-8640

© 2012 Lisa MacDonald. All Rights Reserved.

No part of this book may be reproduced, stored in a retrieval system,
or transmitted by any means without the written permission of the author.

Published by AuthorHouse 11/17/2012

ISBN: 978-1-4772-7948-9 (sc)
978-1-4772-7950-2 (e)

Library of Congress Control Number: 2012919122

Any people depicted in stock imagery provided by Thinkstock are models,
and such images are being used for illustrative purposes only.
Certain stock imagery © Thinkstock.

This book is printed on acid-free paper.

Because of the dynamic nature of the Internet, any web addresses or links contained in this book may have changed
since publication and may no longer be valid. The views expressed in this work are solely those of the author and do not
necessarily reflect the views of the publisher, and the publisher hereby disclaims any responsibility for them.

authorHOUSE®

For my sister Sharon, who enthusiastically encouraged me to read bedtime stories.

Luke and Owen are brothers. Luke is older and is already pretty smart about most things. Owen likes to have fun and doesn't worry about stuff. One day the boys were building a castle together when . . .

"Achoo!" Owen sneezed.

"Oh, no! Germ alert!" cried Luke. "Invasion, invasion! Quick Owen, put the soldiers inside the castle!"

"What invasion?" asked Owen.

"You sneezed out your yucky germs and now they are all over the place," said Luke.

"Where? I can't see them," questioned Owen.

"They are there, but they are too tiny for us to see. Next time cover your sneeze please. The soldiers and I don't want to breathe in your germs and get your cold," explained Luke.

"Okay," agreed Owen.

"Wahoo! We are out! Let's be on the lookout for someone else to give a cold to

because that's what we do! Ha, ha! Hee, hee!" laughed the germs.

"Achoo!" Owen sneezed again, but this time he sneezed into his hand.

"Alright!" cheered the germs. Hopefully this hand will touch a lot of things and we'll get picked up by another hand. Then if that hand touches an eye, a nose, or a mouth, we'll try to make another cold."

"Owen!" groaned Luke.

"Yes?" asked Owen innocently.

"Now the germs are on your hand," said Luke.

"So? You told me to cover my sneeze," defended Owen.

"You'll get germs on anything you touch now, like the blocks. I am playing with them too and I don't want those guys on me. Next time cover your sneeze with your elbow like this," instructed Luke.

"Yeah! Then I can trap the germs in my elbow. That will keep you and our castle safe!"

"Right. Now I command you to squash the germs on your hand with the germ gel in the bathroom," said Luke.

"Yes, Sir," Owen said seriously. He had an important job to do.

Owen pumped hand sanitizer onto his palm and rubbed his hands together. He wondered what the germs that he couldn't see looked like.

"Ouch, we are losing our germ power!" squealed the germs.

"Look, Owen. I added this tower," said Luke proudly.

"Awesome!" Owen admired. Then he felt something wet dripping out of his nose. He wiped it away.

"Owen!" yelled Luke.

"What?"

"Ew! Now you have germy slime on your fingers!"

"There are germs in my nose drips?" asked Owen.

"Yeah, Owen. You are supposed to use a tissue for your nose drips. Go blow the rest of them out," ordered Luke. "And then wash your hands really well."

Owen was on another mission; he went back to the bathroom, got a tissue, and blew all of the germy slime out of his nose.

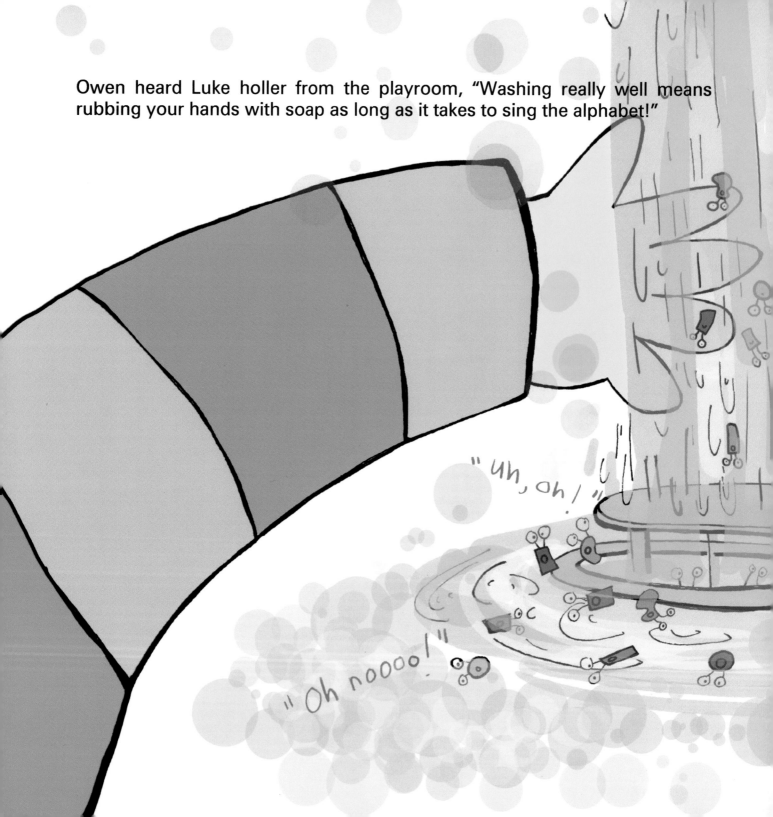

Owen heard Luke holler from the playroom, "Washing really well means rubbing your hands with soap as long as it takes to sing the alphabet!"

"A B C D E F G H I J K L M N O P Q R S T U V W X Y and Z," sang Owen. All cleaned up, Owen quietly tiptoed back to the playroom and . . .

"Boo!" yelled Owen.

Luke jolted with surprise. "Ah! . . . That was a good one, Owen," he giggled.

"Let's make the dungeon now," suggested Owen. He felt a scratchy tickle in his throat and he coughed.

"OWEN!"

"Now, what?"

"You just got your yucky germs on Drake!" cried Luke with frustration.

"The germs are in my coughs too?" asked Owen.

"Yes! Cough into your elbow just like you would do with a sneeze," demanded Luke with exasperation.

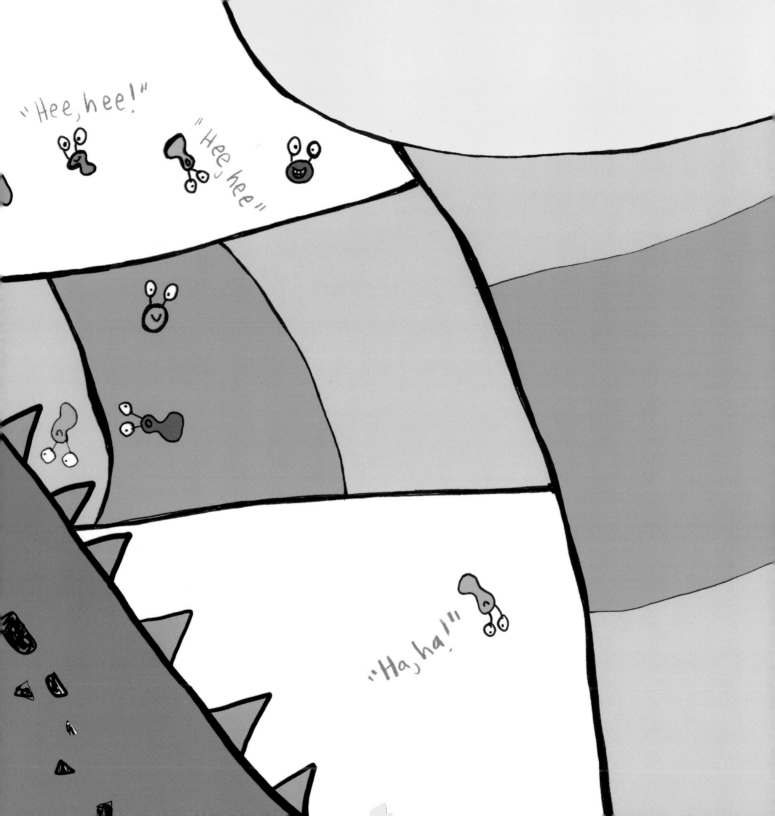

"Time to wash up for snack, boys," called Mom. "We'll be leaving for Luke's Tae Kwon Do class soon."

The boys raced to the sink. Luke got there first because he is older and has longer legs to run with. Luke washed off the germs that he might have gotten on his hands while playing. And Owen washed off the germs that he coughed onto his hand while holding Drake.

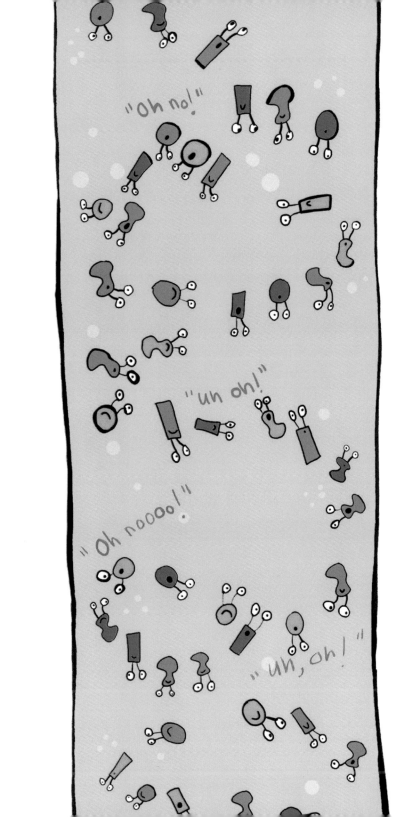

The boys were excited to have their favorite snack: fruit slices and yogurt. Luke was very hungry and began eating right away.

Owen took his time. "I made a rhino with my fruit," said Owen with delight.

"Cool!"

"Did you finish building the castle that you've been working on?" asked Mom.

Luke answered, "Not yet. We had to stop and hide the soldiers inside the castle because of Owen's germ invasions."

"Maybe we can let them out after Tae Kwon Do class," suggested Owen.

"Only if you promise not to cause another germ invasion," said Luke. "I don't want to get sick. And the soldiers can't get sick and miss the big battle. I'm going to get changed."

Owen felt a little bit of tingling in his nose. The sensation was getting stronger and stronger. It was a sneeze building up strength!

"Achoo!"

"Yeah, I finally did it right!" exclaimed Owen happily.

"Hiyah! Can't get me, germs!"

Note to Caregivers about the Rhinovirus
aka: The Common Cold

Since we can't see germs, we often forget about them until we get sick. Then our body sneezes and coughs to expel the irritating germs. The nose also produces mucous and becomes "runny" to flush them out. Therefore, it's very important to minimize the exposure of these droplets to surrounding, healthy people. Use these tips every day to keep healthy and minimize the spread of germs.

- Cough and sneeze into your elbow.

- Do not invite germs in to play by touching your eyes, nose, or mouth.

- Wash your hands before snacks and meals.

- Keep tissues and hand sanitizer handy wherever you go.

- Avoid sharing food, drink, and toothpaste.

- Reward children with praise for practicing good hygiene.

- Model these behaviors and children will develop healthy habits too.

Be well!

Lisa Lynn MacDonald lives, loves, and laughs with her husband, Michael, and her two sons, Luke and Owen, in Hopkinton, MA. One of her many treasured experiences of motherhood is the time she spent reading to Luke and Owen at bedtime. How wonderful it was to snuggle with them and take in the joyful journey that books took them on. Lisa was so impressed by the extent to which books positively influenced her children's development, that she was inspired to write down a little story from bits and pieces that occurred in her home to share with the world. Lisa hopes that **Can't Get Me!** will entertain and enlighten your children, and help them to live life with wellness.

Madison Mastrangelo grew up in Millis, MA and studied Animation at Massachusetts College of Art and Design. She is currently a freelance illustrator and an art teacher. Madison is also the illustrator of *My Adventures with Terry the Bear,* a bedtime story for Hotel Commonwealth in Boston, MA. For the art inspiration of **Can't Get Me!**, she thought of her younger brother Brett, who was always coughing and sneezing growing up. Madison would like to thank Lisa MacDonald for the opportunity, and her family, Karen, Ken and Brett for their love and support. Madison's personal and professional work can be found on her website: madisonmastrangelo.com